Kevin the Unicorn

It's not All Rainbows

Jessika von Innerebner

Dial Books for Young Readers

To anyone who's had a bad day

Dial Books for Young Readers
An imprint of Penguin Random House LLC, New York

Copyright © 2019 by Jessika von Innerebner

Visit us online at penguinrandomhouse.com

Library of Congress Cataloging-in-Publication Data
Names: Von Innerebner, Jessika, author, illustrator.
Title: Kevin the unicorn : it's not all rainbows / Jessika von Innerebner.
Other titles: It's not all rainbows Description: New York : Dial Books for Young Readers, [2019] |
Summary: Even sparkly unicorns that are filled with magical awesomeness and
bring glitter and happiness to everything around them can have a bad day.
Identifiers: LCCN 2018058575 | ISBN 9781984814302 (hardcover)
Subjects: | CYAC: Unicorns—Fiction. Classification: LCC PZ7.1.V677 Ke 2019 | DDC [E]—dc23
LC record available at https://lccn.loc.gov/2018058575

Printed in China · 10 9 8 7 6 5 4 3 2 1

Design by Lily Malcom · Text set in Shag Expert Lounge

Everyone knows unicorns are perfect.

They bring glitter and happiness to everything around them.

Their smiles alone make rainbows appear.

That is how it was for Kevin . . .

until the morning he woke up on the floor.

This had never happened before.
Something felt different.

Something WAS different!
But Kevin knew just what to do.

KEEP IT HAPPY,
he reminded himself.

ALWAYS REMEMBER TO Smile

With an extra-big smile,
Kevin set out for a glittery and fantastic day.

Sure, his day had started off on the wrong hoof,
but Kevin was positive he could turn it around.

However, things did not go as planned .

SMILING
PINES
TRAILS

HAPPY!!

SODA
SHACK

By the time he got to town, Kevin felt a little frazzled.
He'd never had a less-than-perfect morning.

KEEP IT HAPPY, Kevin told himself.

Maybe a Glitter Soda would get his day back on track!

HOLY HOOVES!

The line was long, but Kevin was sure it would move quickly.

It didn't, though.
And by the time he got to the front, they were out of Glitter Soda!

KEEP IT HAPPY,

he said to himself.

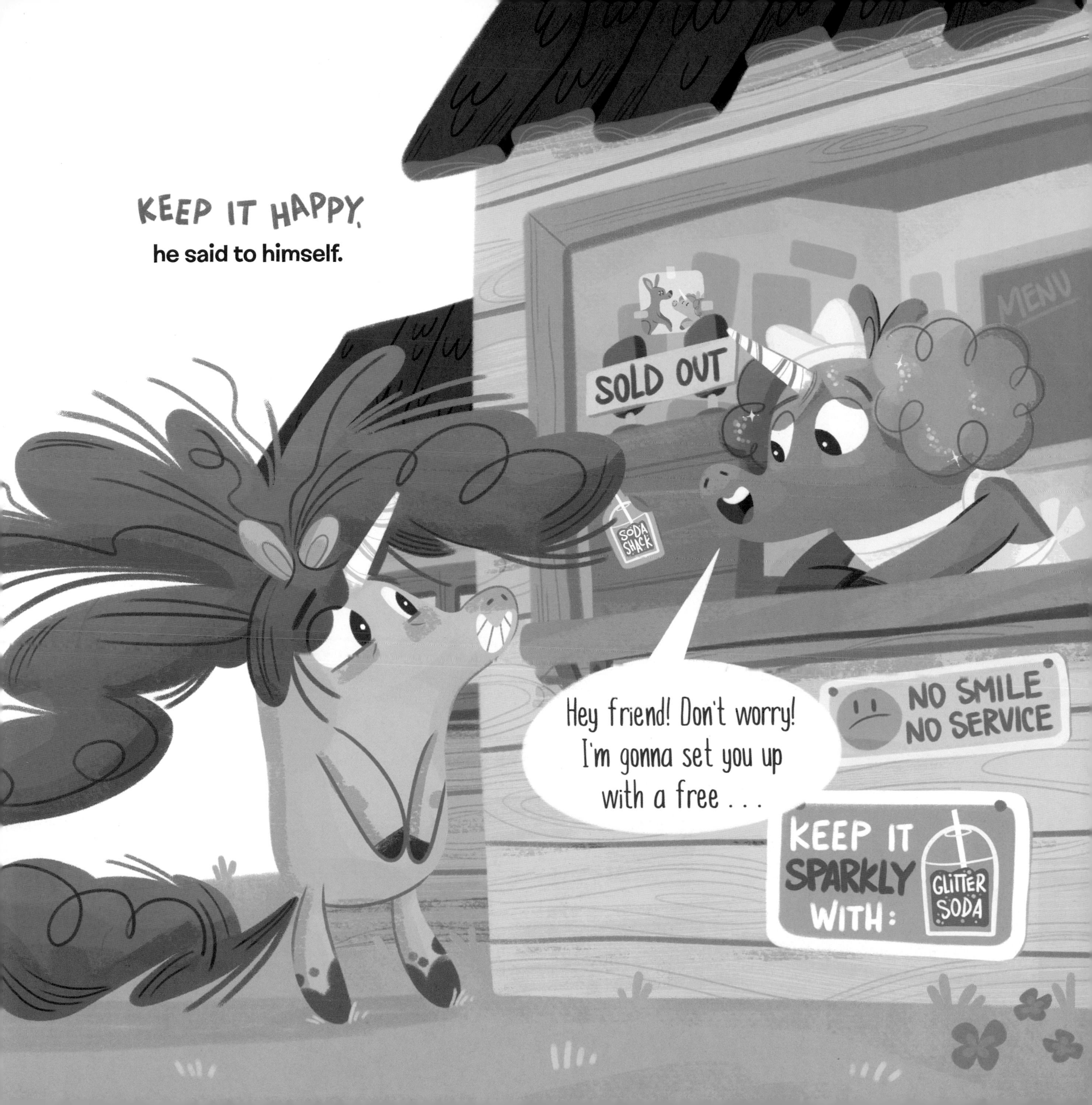

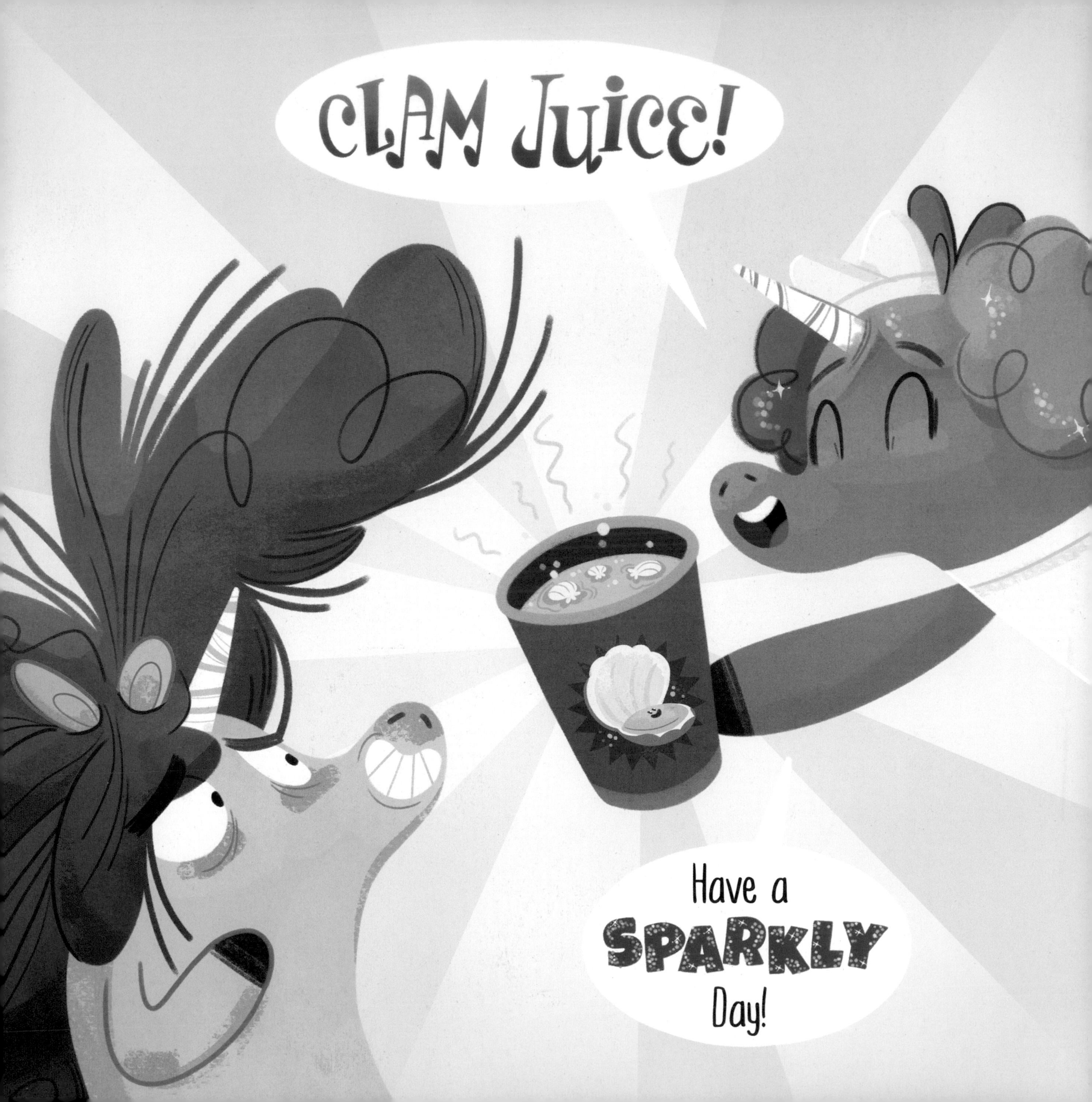
CLAM JUICE!
Have a SPARKLY Day!

WHAT A HAPPY DAY!

ALWAYS BE A HAPPY-CORN

GOT SMiLES?

Kevin kept a smile on his face
even though his insides
didn't feel smiley at all.

Kevin could no longer hide what he was really feeling.

...There's clam juice on my favorite shirt.
SMILE
This has been stuck on my horn for a week and I've been pretending it's not there.

It turns out unicorns don't always have perfect, magical days.

And that's okay.